MOS EISLEY MAZE

Han and Chewie are in
trouble and need your
help! Go to pages 4-5
and lead them to safety.

STAR WARS

JEDI FORCE

WATCH OUT FOR THE WOOKIEE

Han Solo and his trusty Wookiee friend, Chewbacca, are on a mission – a mission to escape the stormtroopers who are closing in on them!
"Looks like trouble," Han tells Chewie. "Let's get out of here!"
"Aawrr!" agrees Chewie.

"Follow me," Han assures his pal. "I know my way around!"

Han leads Chewie through the spaceport of Mos Eisley.

Han and Chewie finally reach the *Millennium Falcon*.
"See?" Han asks. "Just where I left it. Now let's get going!"
"Rowrr!" Chewie protests.

"The hyperdrive?" Han asks. "Of course I checked it. Don't worry so much. Nobody knows this ship better than me!"
"Aargh?" Chewie questions.
"Of course I'm sure!" Han replies. "She's running perfectly. Now let's go!"

In the cockpit, Han leans back, resting his hands behind his head.
"See, Chewie? I've got everything under control – as usual."

Suddenly, an Imperial Star Destroyer closes in on the *Falcon*.
"Uh-oh," Han warns. "Looks like we have company! Jump to lightspeed!"

Chewie lets out a nervous howl.
"What do you mean the hyperdrive isn't working?! Try it again!" yells Han.
But Chewie's right. It isn't working!

Chewie quickly spots a nearby planet. "Raawrr!"
"Got it, Chewie! We're going in, but it's going to be a rough landing.
Hang on!" Han replies.

Han safely lands the *Millennium Falcon* in a clearing in the forest.

"I think we're safe for now," Han says. "There's no one around for miles."

Chewie looks at Han. "Raargh!"
"What do you mean you told me so!? And anyway, I can fix the hyperdrive in less time than it takes to say 'Wookiee'," Han answers.
Han opens a hatch and a pile of tools lands on his head. "Oww!" he yelps.

Chewie laughs. "Laugh it up, fuzzball!" Han snaps.
"Aaugh!" Chewie responds.
"Fine!" Han yells. "I'll fix this myself – without your help! Go ahead – get out of here – and stay out of trouble!"

Chewie throws up his hairy arms and walks away.

Han quickly gets to work, trying to repair the hyperdrive.
"I can fix it myself!" he grumbles.

Meanwhile, outside the *Millennium Falcon*, stormtroopers surround the ship. They quietly make their way inside and capture Han.

Escorted out in handcuffs, Han mumbles under his breath, "I sure could use a Wookiee right now."

Suddenly, a familiar howl fills the air…

…and an entire army of Wookiees comes out of the woods, surrounding the stormtroopers.
Chewie leads the way!

The Wookiees close in on the stormtroopers and lead them away into the forest.

Chewie looks down at Han. "Roww!"
"I know, I know," Han replies. "But first, get me out of these handcuffs!"

Back inside the ship, Chewie calmly fixes the hyperdrive.

"Thanks, Chewie," says Han. "Looks like I needed your help after all."

The *Millennium Falcon* takes off, shifting into hyperdrive.
"And I guess you are pretty smart..." admits Han. "...for a fuzzball!"
"Aawgrh!"

STAR WARS
JEDI FORCE

A GALAXY FULL OF ADVENTURE AWAITS IN *STAR WARS* JEDI FORCE! JOIN LUKE SKYWALKER, HAN SOLO, DARTH VADER AND ALL YOUR OTHER FAVORITE *STAR WARS* CHARACTERS FOR FUN ON EITHER SIDE OF THE FORCE!

COLLECT THEM ALL!

Yoda™ & Luke Skywalker™

R2-D2™ & C-3PO™

Stormtrooper™ & Darth Vader™

Jar Jar Binks™ & Anakin Skywalker™

Anakin Skywalker's Jedi Starfighter™ with R2-D2™

Freeco Bike™ with Obi-Wan Kenobi™

Landspeeder™ with Luke Skywalker™

Snowspeeder™ with Luke Skywalker™ & Han Solo™

WWW.PLAYSKOOLHEROES.COM

GET IN ON THE ADVENTURE AND COLLECT THEM ALL!

STAR WARS JEDI FORCE

WATCH OUT FOR THE W...

TRANSFORMERS RESCUE BOTS

RAPID RESCUE

Books only available in playsets. Playsets sold separately.

MARVEL SUPER HERO ADVENTURES

SPIDEY'S PUMPKIN PROBLEMS

PLAYSKOOL HEROES

WWW.PLAYSKOOLHEROES.COM

711702000

PLAYSKOOL HEROES